Never Stop Dreaming

Flairs and Glairs

Publication House

Disclaimer

This is a work of fiction and solely represent the thoughts of the corresponding authors of the articles. Our editors have tried their best to edit the content of all the authors and check the plagiarism.

All the write-ups in this book are unique and are only published in this book.

In case any plagiarism or error is found, only the author is responsible alone, and not the publisher or the Compilers.

Cover Designing and Book Formatting
Shubham Shah and Ishani Agarwal

Acknowledgement

We would like to thank for everything, is our families. We don't think without your support, anything would have been possible.

Our families did everything they could, to make sure we follow our passion.

As per this book, we would thank is Shivangi di without whose support and guidance, this wouldn't have been possible. Shubham Shah, the owner of the publishing house, thank you for helping and supporting the way you did.

Shubham Shah & Shivangi Jaiswal, without your support, we wouldn't have been standing here.

Lastly, the most important thank you note goes to my Co-Authors. Had you not supported us, and helped us in this journey by being so patient, we wouldn't have been able to get this ready in such a short span of time

Co Author

Shubham Shah (Founder Flairs and Glairs)
Ishani Agarwal (Co-Founder Flairs and Glairs)
Shivangi Jaiswal (Project Head)
Muskan A. Mulla (Compiler)
Nishiket R Surwade (Compier)

1. Jaishree Suresh
2. Palak Binzode
3. Purva Mestry Ingale
4. Srishti Singh
5. Shiyona Das
6. Lipsa Sahoo
7. Samiksha
8. Nidhi Verma
9. Shivam Sahu
10. Shravan Panchal
11. Saloni Lal Shrivastava
12. Navjyot Verma
13. Reshma Samnani
14. Dr.Manjusha Hari
15. Kapil Sahare
16. Surender Saini
17. Harkirat Singh

Shubham Shah

(Founder- Flairs and Glairs)

Shubham Shah, an entrepreneur at "Flairs & Glairs" a brand with dynamics in events organizing and cultural educational pan INDIA, is a 26yrs old guy who recently has entered the digital platform of imprinting emotions. He has initiated with his own open mic platform to help budding poets and aspiring writers under his brand named as "Teekhe Zasbaaat"

He is a commerce graduate from the Bhagalpur City of Bihar. He states Writing has impersonated him since childhood and he has now been writing for over a decade!
Cooking, on the other hand, is his passion! He also mentions, trying out new things just tickles him!
When asked sir, Why SPICY EMOTIONS?
He smiled and added, "agar jasbaat teekhe na ho toh wo jasbaat kahan" Spices are all that blends! So do his words!
As a chef, he presents to you his dish! Hot and freshly served! Taste it! Feel it! Enjoy it! You can also find his writing in the Book "Teekhe Zasbaaat" and 50+ Co-authored anthologies. With his passion to explore opportunities across Platforms, he is working with keen devotion and We wish him all the very best for his future ventures.
He is Featured in the International Magazine DeMode for his upcoming solo novel.
He is Approved by Ne8x for its Lit Fest, and is a Golden Star Awards 2020 Winner.
He is a India Book of Records Holder for his Anthology Satrang, and has the Grandmaster title by Asia Book of Records, for the same.
He has also been featured in Prabhat Khabar, Dainik Jagran, and a lot of other Newspapers in Bihar for his achievements.
He has been a proud co-author to
India Book Of Records (Title- Black)
World Book Of Records (Title -15 Wonders of Poetries)
India Book Of Records (Title - Aaina)
Vajra World Records Holder (Title - Gustakhi Maaf Hai)
High Range of Records Holder (Title - Gustakhi Maaf Hai)
Indian Book of Records
(Title - Road from Worst to Best)

Share your reviews on his

INSTAGRAM
@spicy_emotions
@shubham4shah
Or via email on
shubham2shah@gmail.com

To stay tuned to his work and opportunities follow his business Handles

INSTAGRAM   FACEBOOK   YOUTUBE

@flairsandglairs
@teekhezasbaaat

WEBSITE:
https://flairsandglairs.in/
https://flairsandglairs.com/

Ishani Agarwal

(Co-Founder- Flairs and Glairs)

Ishani Agarwal hails from the City of Joy, Kolkata.
She is the co-founder of her Community "Teekhe Zasbaaat" and Flairs and Glairs Publication.
Been a Compiler for 45+ Anthologies, she is in the process for more. Co-authored in 150+ Anthologies. She is a India Book of Records Holder, a Vajra World Records Holder, a High Range of Records Holder, an OMG Book of Records Holder, a Bravo Record holder, a Forever Star Book of World Records and an Indian Book of Records Holder.
Approved by Ne8x for its Lit Fest 2020, and Literary Icon 2020. Also a Golden Star Awards Winner 2020.
She has also been awarded with India Star Republic Award 2021, a part of She Awards by Awards Arc and Winner of Nari Samman 2021 by Literoma.

She is also selected as Best Achiever of the Year by AwardsArc and Most Challenging Compiler Award by Spectrum Awards.
She got her first solo Published,a solo Compilation consisting of first 750 contents of hers, titled "Hand That Burnt While Healing".

She has been featured by the National Magazine "Taree Zameen Par" with the title 'unstoppable'.
Also featured in the International Magazine DeMode for her upcoming solo novel, she is proud to write on social issues, and is happy with the love she is receiving.
Connect with her on Instagram: @Ishani_agarwal_quotes / @compilations_so_far

Shivangi Jaiswal
(Project Head)

Shivangi Jaiswal is a Content Writer from Kolkata. She is a B. Com Honours graduate. Certified in Stocks & Short Selling as well as Certified in Digital Marketing. Been a keen student, she has recently been Certified for learning Spanish Language. She is a writer by day and a reader by night. Been a Complier of 30+ Anthologies, and in process for more, also Co- authored 120+ anthologies. Shivangi is an old soul with young eyes, a vintage heart, and a beautiful mind."

You can follow her work:

Instagram

@the_knockingvibe

@house_of_compilations

Don't Quit.

Things go wrong, sometimes they will.
When the road you are taking seems to drift.
Smile, Yes Smile and walk forward.
Because when you want to touch the sky.
Quitting is never an option.

Life is always with twists and turns.
As everyone is here to learn
Many times, we fail.
Many times, we win but we are struck out.
So never lose hope.

Often strugglers give up.
When they are just a few steps away from their winning.
But you don't give up.
Never, because you, yes you sitting there you are a warrior and warriors never give up.

Success is all about failure turning into success.
So, stick to the fight and give the hardest hit.
Because things seem worse.

There is a saying which says: A Coal also turns into a Diamond one day.

And yes, we are the gems sitting here with the Brightest future.

Muskan A. Mulla
(Compiler)

Let me introduce you to the Writer
Miss: Muskan A. Mulla
Born on 17th December 1998
She is a Final year Student Pursuing her Degree in Bachelor of Computer Application, Bhatkal, Karnataka.
She is Very Shy and Simple.
Her Hobbies are Sketching, Painting, Travelling, crafts, Reading Books and Writing Poetry's.
She Started writing since past 1 Year.
She Loves to Write Poetry's, Quotes, short lines, micro Tales. In English, Hindi, and Hinglish.
She Worked as a Co-Author in Some Anthologies and Never Stop Dreaming is her First Anthology as a Compiler.

Akhir Kya..?

Akhir Kya haii tujhme aisa jo hume kheenchta hai teri taraf,
Akhir kya hai tujhme aisa jo hume yoon tootne nahi deta,
Akhir kya hai tujhme Aisa jo hume aur hosla deta haii,
Akhir kya haii tujhme aisa jo hume yoon bikharne nahi deta,
Akhir kya haii tujhme aisa jo chand ki chandni bhi tujhpe fida haii,
Akhir kya haii tujhme aisa
Akhir Kya..?

Aane wala kal

Hum Sab kahi na kahi aaj bhi khudko uss beete hue kal ki aag me jala rahe hain
Yeh bhi na socha ki
Woh toh guzra hua kal tha Aaj nahii
Woh toh guzra hua kal tha aaj nahi,
Jab ki Aane waala kal toh Phool Bichaye hue hamara khushiyon ke saath intezaar kar raha haii.

Kashmakash

Aaj Yeh Dil Me Kaisi Kashmakash haii
Yeh Dil Uljha bhi haii toh uske khayalon me haii,
Jise abhi takk iski khabar hi nahi.

Nishiket R Surwade
(Compiler)

Mr.Nishiket R Surwade,born on 24th july 1999 .
He is a student pursuing his engineering in electronics and telecommunication field, Nashik, Maharashtra & Also a Project Co- Ordinator at "Flairs & Glairs"He is very shy and simple, easily make friends. He is a blogger and future E&TC engineer. He aspires to become IAS Officer.
He has started writing as a career since he was in 12th std.He loves to write quote and shayri in Hindi as well as in English language. He loves to write about 'True love'
He worked as co-author in some anthologies like
'The Broken Bond', 'For the name of love' and in more than 50 Anthologies. and also, being a compiler of the book "College Romance", "Life Sahi Hai" and many are
in process

Main Hoon Na

Kuchh iss kadar dono rishta nibhayenge,
Ki samjhdari tum dikhana nadani ke liye ,
Main hoon na.

Tum gusse main ruth jaya karna,
Tumhe manane ke liye,
Main hoon na.

Gusse main mujhe daant liya karna tum,
Tumhari mithi si daant sunne ke liye,
Main hoon na.

Thak jaao ya pad jaao bimar to,
Tumhara khayal rakhne ke liye,
Main hoon na.

Agar kabhi bata na sako to,
Sidha jata dena haq,
Tumhe samjhane ke liye,
Main hoon na….

Jaishree

About Yourself (3rd person format) *
A medico student who is passionate about writing. Writing is her only expression be it happiness or sadness. 21 year old aspires to be a poet one day so that she could touch people's heart.

(1)

The very first time you gazed at me,
I was busy with my own self you must agree.
About 6:00pm message popped up on my phone,
A message I should have ignored and thrown .
But.......
Your message made my senses blew away...
Wooh...
I have been always taught "stay away from strangers and trust nobody".
But you were more than an unknown known person to me.
It seemed addictive.
Little did I know that I have been preyed,
For you I was a new toy to play
And for me technically you were my first love.
You won my heart without even having a battle,
And I lost it without even having a fight.
With your cheesy talks,
Clowny walks , chocolate thoughts
And bitter truths..
I was falling more and more for you.
You were having your popcorn bite,
When I was thinking of you the whole night ,
You were kissing someone else under the moon,
And I was still waiting for you like a fool.
Months passed,
And you felt this toy to be old and boring.
The heart that was filled with love,
You filled it all with venom .
And interestingly one fine day you left this toy all alone .
Technically it was my first love,
It was difficult to forget you ,
But seemed easy to forgive you,

Months passed with depression and mood swings.
After months the toy caterpillar turned out to be a butterfly,
Becoming someone unimaginable.
Now , I understand
That love was never meant to be mine,
And now I am totally fine .
With my wings wide open.
And door for everyone all closed.
Because
when you are kind to yourself,
You can be kind to others.

If ever you need me I'll be there in your heart.

Palak Binzode.

I Started Writing At The Age Of 19, I Feel
Good And Relaxed After Writing, And It Is My Passion Now
And I Love Writing..

(1)

भीनी भीनी सी मुस्कान तेरी,
जैसे महक लुभान की लुभाती हो,
रौनक ऐसी चेहरे की,
जैसे चढ़ती चादर दरगाह को सजाती हो,
रंगरेज़ हैं तेरी आंखे ऐसी,
जैसे रात को काली रँगाती हों,
रोशन हैं आसमा खूशबू से उसकी,
जैसे खुदा को दावत पे रोज़ बुलाती हो।

(2)

जिंदगी के तजुर्बों से पार हो जाऊ,
मसले हाल कर हर हालात मे ढल जाऊ,

चाँद सी ठंडक भले ही ना हो मुझमे,
पर टूटते तारे सी दुआ बन जाऊ।

सपने।

क्या होते हैं सपने,
दिलों के तार होते है सपने
दिल जुड़ जाये तो पार होते हैं सपने

उन थकती आंखों का हाल होते हैं सपने,
जिनकी दुआओ से तर होते हैं सपने,

ज़िन्दगी की बुनियाद होते हैं सपने,
बच्चे के पहले अक्षर का प्रमाण होते है सपने,

जो पुरे हो या ना हो,
जिंदगी जीने की आश होते हैं सपने,

जुनून होते हैं सपने,
रूहानियत सा सुकून होते हैं सपने,

किसी की छनकती चाल होते हैं सपने
किसी की खनकती मुस्कान होते हैं सपने
कुछ पाने का अरमान होते है सपने।

Purva Mestry Ingale

She is a French teacher by profession. She has always been passionate towards writing. She started writing at the age of 12 years. She has been publishing on her blog (www.talltales1.wordpress.com) on and off since the past eight years now. Her blog was featured on Baggout as one of the top 15 creative writing blogs in India. She has also been awarded as Literary Colonel on storymirror.com and one of her poems was featured in their ebook anthology. Recently, she has started a dedicated instagram account forher writing called @tallertales1 She tries to portray a deeper perspective into everyday things and aims at creating a change through it. A believer in spreading positivity, she wants to use her writing to do so.

Trust

It's a simple five letter word.
Yet it has the strength of the world.
It needs to be handled with care.
Like a piece of glass.
Trust once broken can never be joined.
But that is not the worst.
If it cracks, the scars of pain remain for a lifetime.
So nurture and protect the trust you have.
Because if it's alive its strength can move mountains and shake
the sky.

With You By My Side

O Peace! You are so very far from me.
How have I erred?
Why do you seem to elude me?

Have you been pushed away?
Shoved into oblivion by negativity?

I know its force is hard.
It has been growing stronger lately.

But we have to face it.
We need to fight it together.

You can't be buried so easily.
Don't let this negativity bully you constantly.

Come join me,
As I lock horns with this pessimistic ideology.

I am going to battle till I win you back.
Either alone or with you by my side.

(3)

My plants are dead
Withered in the cold,
With no sunlight to grow
But I don't mind at all

The only sound I hear is
The distant snore of my father.
And the scratches of my pencil on paper
As it etches the words on.

To many,
This silence may be deathly.
But not me,
It's a melody that my heart covets

I don't mind this cold wintery air,
But I mind the frost
That it has created
Amongst loved ones

It has made us drift apart
And made us take our separate ways
Our home is the same
But the silence has been butchering the warmth
The warmth in our relationships.

I have new relations to build
Many promises to fulfil
But please don't make break
The old one's made to you.

Srishti Singh

This is Srishti Singh from Raipur Chhattisgarh.... She is an Engineer and she writes occassionally when in mood
You can see more of her writeups on instagram on writer._.on._.mood

Her

Don't mistake her silence
With what u think is weak
She's not easy to seek
Wait for the right time
And keep away ur dirty beak
'cause she'll make u dumb
When she decides to speak......

Sometimes

It's very hard to move on
But once you move on you'll realize
It was the best decision you've made

Ego

We were close like no one
Then a storm came
And drifted us apart
The storm was nthng
But his ego

Shiyona Das

Hey readers!!! She is Miss. Shiyona Das from Bhilai C. G., she is a brilliant nursing student and an inspirational writer, you can read her more on her Instagram page soul_.creations

(1)

KEEP GOING- Don't stop trying even if you failed too many times , Be courageous and trust your hardworkship....

(2)

DREAM SUCESSES- Not all dreams are fantacies some of them can lead you to the peak from where you have powers to change the wrongs.

(3)

NEW DAY NEW LIFE- Every new day is another chance to change your life so make your thoughts fly high and vision deep down.

Lipsa Sahoo

Lipsa Sahoo, a student of Vyasanagar Autonomous College, Jajpur Road, Odisha. She is pursuing her graduation in English honours. She had started writing just after the completion of her 12th board examination. She aims to come across millions of hearts through her words. She says that, she is grateful to her father for his continuous efforts, support, care and infinite love towards her.

Insta Handle: lipsa_sahoo.01

Thoughts For Life

Each morning a new installation.
Forget the deceased yesterday.
It will never wake up.
Its already buried deep inside.

Noone have seen tomorrow.
Its just ambiguous.
But its only in our hands.
Our tomorrow is ushered by today.

Focus on the animate present.
Dream for a intense tomorrow.
Strive and strive to achieve your goal.
Never split trust from self-work.

Never head behind,
in the journey of life.
Because a moving cart wheel,
never spins backward.

Quotes:

* The day you realize the reason behind your presence in this world, is the day you start your journey towards your goal in life.

* Never keep expectations from others, rather make yourself so strong with the flow of time that others will start keeping expectations from you.

* One life changing value that my parents inculcated in me, while growing up is to keep patience and have self-confidence.
Title (writeup 3)
Quotes:

* My roots inspire me to stand athletic and grow with full of credence to outstretch the sky.

* I feel happy when, I see the enamel of paradise in my father's eyes ascribed to my victory.

* My gut tells me to hide my tears of the past miseries behind my eyes and to act actively in the present form, to make my Dad live happily.

Nidhi Verma

Nidhi Verma has been writing various articles, short stories as well as poems for over seven years. Her educational background in Civil Engineering, her curiosity, and passion for writing has given her a broad base from which to approach various topics. Her writings have won in CSVTU essay writing and also published in Kathaclub. She has taken her training in creative writing from Internshala by one of India's leading writers. She works as a freelance writer with several organizations.

VIOLET (This is a story close to my heart and soul. It is going to be the first self published creation of mine and this is just a start. I hope the readers enjoy the story.)

CHARACTER SKETCH (Violet is a 20-year-old student with an unfortunate habit of bumping off the people around her. She is humble and kind-hearted, but can also be very inner darkness and a bit under-confident. She is a French who believes in god. She is currently at college studying law. Physically, Violet is in pretty good shape. She is average-height with light skin, curly black hair, and black eyes. She has soft and chubby cheeks that looked as if they were always filled with sweets. Simplicity is her specialty and it is one of many reasons that many people are attracted to her and she was always loved by everyone she met. Violet always likes to dress light and simple, but she also looks amazing in fancy dresses and she always keeps her hair braided. What Monshu, her elder brother loves most in her simplicity is that she is honest and never tries to impress others for any reason.

Violet comes from a middle-class neighborhood. She has many friends with whom she shares "hard as nail" friendship. She loves spending time with her loved ones as much as she could while deep down inside she is afraid of losing any of them for any reason and fears from the thought of being let down by her own. Violet always wants someone as her company as she is afraid of being alone but hardly shares her fears and emotions with anyone.)

STORY (It was 9:10 in the morning, the sun was not very high and it was a beautiful day. The Parisian parks, early morning movie, tourist spots were already open. Fresh windy cool air and the chirping of birds made a tempting atmosphere and green-brown beautiful countless leaves danced welcoming the morning. By degrees, cafés, shops, galleries, studios, bookstores began to be enclosed. People were getting ready for the day- most for work, tourists for their Paris tours, and students were out to reach their schools and colleges on time.

"How much time do we have?" Stella asked Violet while tying her shoelaces.

"No time at all you idiot," said Violet irking and rushing as she walked towards the exit of the apartment, "we are already 10 minutes late".

"Take it, easy girl! It's not that late to get worried. You should greet me Bonjour but instead, you are yelling at me." Stella taunted.

"No, I won't because you always keep annoying me," Violet said jokingly in a rude tone.

"Ok all done now let's go to the college."

"Sure. We should move fast or else professor Gabriel would not allow us into his class-"

"Don't worry stupid, even if it's a law college he won't throw us inside a jail," Stella said laughing.

"Isn't Talon joining us?"

"I don't know I couldn't contact him."

As they hastened some distance they came to a huge arc entrance of the college gate with fancy design surrounded by some trees and many flower plants and show plants.

"Here we are! Now we won't be thrown out from the class, god saved us." Violet said in relief.

"You and your worries.. See there they are-" Stella pointed towards Talon and Mahieu as they followed them very slowly.

Violet, Stella, Talon, and Mahieu were very close friends and shared very strong emotional bonds even though they were not childhood friends, they met each other in college for the first time. Mahieu and Talon were very caring, especially for these two girls, and Stella and Violet both were free-spirited.

"It's Mahieu's birthday next month, have you anything in your mind?" Violet bumped Stella while walking.

"Here you go again. How many times I warned you not to do this with me?" Stella stepped ahead of Violet "and till now I have nothing in my mind but we should discuss it with Talon as only boys can understand each other very well." She suggested.

"We will talk to him during lunch". They both agreed as they entered the classroom.

During lunchtime, all the four friends were sitting together doing their lunch.

"Oh god! How could I forget it?" cried Violet.

"What?" the other three seriously looked at her.

"Mahieu I forgot to make the copies of the dual assignment which you and I have to submit in the next lecture to professor Ademar, what should I do now?"

"No problem I will get it done right now as I've already finished my lunch," said Mahieu and walked away instantly.

"Now that's what I wanted," Violet winked at others "now we can freely discuss his birthday plan."

"You notorious girl" Talon continued, "by the way Violet, you should once ask your brother he gives nice suggestions."

Violet exclaimed, "Oh yes that's a great idea, I will ask him today itself."

After her classes, Violet came back home and directly went to her brother's room without even taking off her bags.

"My beloved frère, Monshu," she said as she stared him through the ajar door.

"What brings you here ma petite soeur?" he asked.

"It's Mahieu's birthday, what should we do for him?"

"Umm... let me think- Oui you could gift him something very stylish and expensive- or you could throw him a surprise party."

"Yay frère you are so good. Thanks for the suggestion"

She shared this idea with all her friends and it was decided that they would throw a surprise party for Mahieu so they started preparing for it and invited all of their classmates.

Finally, when his birthday came, everything was ready so they called him.

"Hello," Mahieu said over the phone.

"Dude you need to come to Violet's place," Stella said.

"No I can't," he responded hesitatively.

"Why not? We decided to hang out at her place today."

"I'm sorry I can't come." He ended the call saying this.

They tried to reach out to him but they couldn't reach him. They even went to his home but he was not there.

"How rude he is," Violet got angry, "he should not have done this. He insulted me today" and flounced away.

He did not meet them for the next few days, Violet was still very upset about it and finally, when she met him she shouted a lot at him without getting any answers and just walked away from him very rudely.

"What happened bro?" Talon asked him.

"It's nothing," Mahieu replied in a muffled voice and walked away from them.

Later on, they came to know that Mahieu's close aunt was terminally ill and was critical on his birthday. He hadn't told anyone as he was an introvert and also he didn't want anybody to pity him.

After knowing all these things Violet felt very bad and wanted to talk to him but she could not collect enough courage to go and talk to him. She waited some more time and finally went to him.

"I'm sorry Mahieu."

"It has nothing to do with you why are you even here" he replied "broken threads from knots even after being tied again," he continued "I don't want you to be my friend."

She came to Stella after this "what am I going to do now?" She cried.)

Samiksha

She is Samiksha daughter of Mr. Vinod kumar singla and Mrs.
Champa Rani from Bathinda.
She is a girl from a small area with big dreams. Her life
is all around her family, friends and career. She is
one of them who love to spread smile and Positivity.

Believe in Dreams

When you wake up and feel that your life is wrong, you hate your job or just something is missing in your life it's because you stop dreaming.

Every day it's a new opportunity to make your dreams come true so, don't waste it.

Dreaming is all about finding yourself, finding your goals and live a life that you don't regret. If you stop dreaming you won't truly live and when you get old you will regret the dreams you don't persuade.

If you have a dream, you must fight for it, that dream chooses you so have the courage to grab it. Following your dreams is a hard path but it's the only path. People that have easy lives normally stop dreaming because in their paths they never had to fight hard for what they want. It comes with a price as they will never understand that we live from conquers and never appreciate the full taste of accomplishment.

Stop dreaming makes you a kinda person

There are lots of kinda persons. If you kinda want something you shouldn't expect effortless results. So if you want something hard you should dedicate your life to it. You should want it to every part of yourself, you must wake up thinking about it, dreaming about it, breath it, it should consume all your efforts.

What if I have doubts?

Doubt is like a thief that comes disguised and steal your dreams. Hesitation makes you have a fear of failure and disillusion. If you are chasing your dreams sometimes you will feel like you are failing, disappointed and without strength to continue, but all that is part of the climbing to the top. Don't expect smooth paths to success. And above of everything never give up on what you want.

In your path, there will be mistakes, fears, doubts, stressful moments but even if you make a step behind you should keep going. Don't expect to make it for the first time. You should be persistent, never back down and never surrender.

Hard times prepare people for great futures

Your future starts now and only you can decide it. Don't follow other people dreams and don't let them decide your life. Finding what you love is like finding someone to spend the rest of your life. Your work will be a major part of your life so you

Shravan Panchal

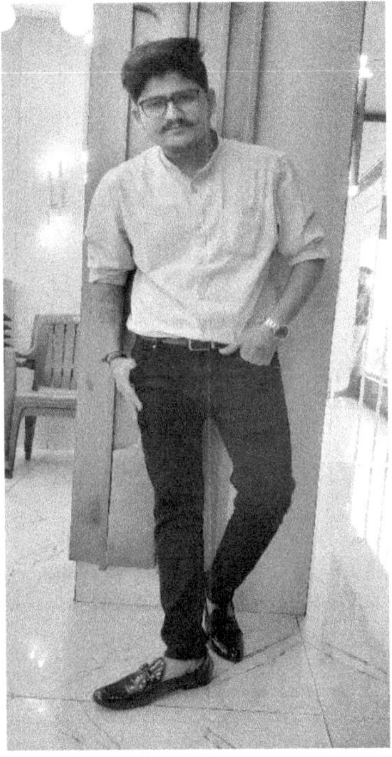

Thecreative_pen claims to be The God. Has Traveled 60% of India. Loves Animals. Has 9 Tattoos. Hates Humans.

(1)

These days i have to bite my thumb,
To make my mind stop from going numb.

(2)

हर पल मैने लिखना चाहा है,
मेरे मन से खुदको,
दूर खींचना चाहा है।

मन मेरा आवारा है,
ज़िंदा रहने के लिए मारा मारा है।

इसे खुशियों में कम्ही ढूंढ़ना आता है,
दुख को बढ़ाने का जरिया बताना आता है।

कोई कुछ कह दे तो उसके,
हजार मतलब निकाल लेगा,
खुदको कभी आराम नहीं देगा।

नींद में भी मुझे डराता है,
जो है ही नहीं उससे मुझे हराता है।

लिखना मुझे इससे आराम देता है,
क्या ये मेरा वहम, मन का बनाया तोह नहीं?

(3)

Finally my mind stoped working.
Heart took the charge.
Spoke about things i never imagined.
I started to feel lost and heavy.
I could feel,
number of nails pierced in my heart.
Still it was beating,
It was hurting but still it was beating.
I tried to remove them, one by one at a time.
It took me a while to remove those nails,
but i did remove them.
Whenever i removed a nail,
it left a hole in my heart.
I noticed something weird,
those hole started to gather,
and made one big hole in my heart.
Day by day it was increasing,
after a while it consumed my whole heart,
and still i was alive.
That hole is my heart now?
Where did my heart go?
Ik only one thing about this hole,
it's created by me only.

Saloni Lal Srivastava

She is Saloni Lal Srivastava daughter of Mr. Kumar Prashant and Mrs. Asha Sinha from Siwan, Bihar
She is pursuing B.sc in Botany honors.She is currently, working as a Social media handler of Teekhe Zasbaaat a writing comunityunder Flairs & Glairs Publication House.Her life is all around her family, friends and career.
She has also worked as co author in 50+
anthologies.She is the one who loves to spread smile andpositivity to everyone.
You can follow her on Instagram:
@salonilalsrivastava.

(1)

Everyone sees a dream and tries to fulfill it .dreams are like magic ,it takes uu to that world where everything happens according to you but when u come back in reality u felt that fulfilling dreams is not that much easier .dreams are those which can't let u sleep .u continuously works towards achieving your goal .some dreams to be an actor ,some dreams to be teacher and some only wanted to have a happy and peaceful life and everyone tries there best to achieve this .like this I also have dream to become an entrepreneur. I want to do something which is related to me ,something unique ,something which is loved by everyone .an idea which looks like magic .so in order to fulfill my dream I opened my own event management company .since childhood I liked to manage events ,decorate places ,functions and all .recently I got a new event to plan .there was some business party happening at a famous celebrity house .I got a chance to meet them .I was so happy as this was the first time I was meeting any famous celebrity like this .I felt like my dreams come true .but there was something missing ..I was not getting that vibe .the magic I want to feel I was not able to feel that .while returning to my house I met a little girl on the signal she was selling balloons .she insisted me to buy one .I was not able to say no .so I bought some .and I felt happy .and this becomes my daily routine meeting that girl everyday on the signal .one day she told me that she is hungry .I took her to one shop and bought her pav bhaji .she was so happy after eating this .she told me that today is her birthday .and she asked me to come to her place .when I reached there with her .I felt that I have to do something for her to make her happy .I called my friend there and we together decorated that little place of her with balloons and sparkles .and brought her a cake .I have never felt this much happy in my life .she was dancing in joy ,running

41

towards to her friends ,calling them.and after that she cut her cake and give me first bite .she was so little but she makes me feel my worth .and this makes me feels that if u truly wanted to fulfill ur dreams ,makes ur surrounding happy ,give things to people who actually needs them .fulfilling your own dream will not give you this much happiness .the real joy of life u will get after fulfilling someone else dream .if u make someone else happy u will see the real magic in your life .and u will feel that u have achieved your every goal ,fulfilled every dream of your life .

Navjyot Verma

Navjyot Verma is a young immature writer who lives in Sambalpur, Odisha. She has recently completed her secondary studies from DAV Public School, Burla and contiguously she is pursuing her hobby of writing. She has been the house leader of the school and even the member of the environment one music club. She is a voracious reader and after every reading collects her thoughts about the book. According to her a great family bond nurtures the creative waters. Her first poem was published in "Khwaabo ka silsila" by Booksquirrel Publication and more of her works are at queue. She is looking forward to present great works in times aheadyou can contact her at- Navjyotreet02@gmail.com

(1)

One should always be ready to live, before we know, the time runs out. Life is a one time offer,one should use it well. When life gives you an opportunity to check on the things on your bucket list, you have to check them. One day life will flash before your eyes and you have to make sure,it's worth watching. Adventure always awaits. We live, we die, the world goes round and round. So, whenever you get a chance,pick up your bag and jump off the cliff, 'cause what counts the life, you live in the years.

~ You need not even listen, just wait...the world will offer itself freely to you, unmasking itself.
The best travelers aren't those who have the fattest wallets, bulkier backpacks but those who have their dream in their eyes and a perfect relaxing travel plan. And when the tour is with your friends, it ought to be action-packed, fun and unforgettable. You are bound to create so many memories together. I've always been interested in visiting different places, whether that's going to the seaside, countryside or going abroad, or even just visiting a new city. I love travelling, well I love being in other places, the travelling part of travelling isn't as fun! Over the years,I've created a Travel Wish List. This list isn't full and there are so many other places I'd love to see, but at the top of these has always been Paris. Fascinated by the city lights and the iconic Eiffel Tower, it has been The City Of Lights, The City Of Love. It has been named so by the people around the world who visit the place and experience the vibes it exudes.

Paris... It has been the dream place of millions,so as is mine. It is always a good option to say a big Yess...!!! I always wanted to go to Paris since I was little just looking at the pictures in magazines makes me so mad that I never went there. From its sun-flecked harbours to its quite mouthwatering cafes, it has a picturesque charm. I want to spend my day enthralling one of the most romantic destinations - the Eiffel Tower and admiring its architectural beauty, spending my day walking down the array of high-end hotels and designer stores which draws in thousands of shoppers every single day. It even plays home to theatres, jewellers, restaurants, cinemas, and nightclubs ! Aside from these, Galeries Lafayette is something which I would want to visit once in a lifetime. This stylish department store is located in a stunning building and offers visitors the chance to purchase designer goods. In case, one is not into shopping much, they can prefer visiting the churches, art galleries and museums in the city. The burg even offers mesmerising gardens which are the best place to amble an afternoon at. Visiting a bookshop is of high priority on my sight-seeing bucket list, so I would rather prefer that in the evening along with some time to relax myself in a cold and calm place. The best things to see in Paris at night, especially when it lights up. The Paris nightlife scene is thriving with vibrant and varied scenes and city lights. Whenever you're looking for something that's a little more than dinner, or you want to head out on the town then the city is famous around the world.

There has been a place we've all been wanting to go for awhile now.One always have a dream to go a tour around the world. A vacation is nothing to do and all day to do it in. No matter what fabulous place one visit, you don't feel like you're on vacation unless you're dehydrated and covered with sunscreen. Chilling out on the bed in your hotel room watching television, while wearing your own pajamas, is sometimes the best part of a vacation and futhermore, vacation calories don't count.

Reshma Samnani

Ms. Samnani has been a part of the incredible teaching fraternity for fifteen years and has taught English Language and Literature across ICSE, ISC, IGCSE, AS/A Levels and IBDP Curricula. Her sincere professional endeavors have constantly fueled her love and passion for writing. Her works revolve mostly around feminism, philosophy, spirituality, justice, racism, distressed, optimism, love and romance.

Lessons From A Withered Tree

Looking Out Of The Window At The Withered Tree Wondered I Why Is It Still Standing Firm And High? I Pitied Its State For It Bore No Fruits Nor Flowers The Leaves, Too, Had Abandoned It Making It Lonely And Desolate The Grief Swallowed Me Thinking If That Would Be Me I Would Have Died Before Death If All I Loved Abandoned Me The Wretched Face, The Bare Branches Made My Heart Sink I Wished It Died Soon For Only Death Could Ease It From Its Shrink But The Undaunted Seed Refused To Weigh Down Its Faith And Continued To Linger On With No Intent To Concede Quietly It Stayed Put In The Dismantled Shape Withstanding All The Hardships Until One Day… A Tiny Leaf Sprouted From One Of Its Branches Like A Silver Lining Striking Amidst The Dark Clouds The Reward Of Endurance It Soon Reaped- The Leaves And The Flowers Embraced The Tree Which Could No More Be Called 'Withered'.

Trapped Swan (Swan – A Metaphor For 'Soul')

Set The Trapped Swan Free
To Feel The Ultimate Bliss

Why Do You Chain It To-
The Quest For Penny
The Hunger For Fame
The Greed For Honor

The Swan Knows Not

The Earthly Bounds;
Limiting It To The Materialistic Fence,
Shall Bring Misery To Your Fate.

The Shiny Armour, The Sharp Sword,
The Scepter, The Crown,
Shall Not Stand The Decay
And Tumble Down.

The Roof You Call Your Home
The Weaves You Call Your Garb
The Mortals You Call Your Love
The Bread You Call Your Need

Shall Betray You And Not
Follow On The Journey
Beyond. Beyond This Myth,
There's A Real World.
Beyond This Illusion,
There's A Truth.
Beyond This Turmoil,
There's Certainty.
Beyond This Mundane,
There's Divinity.

Awake! Act! Before It's Too Late!
Your Swan Belongs Not Here
Deter Not Its Flight On The Virtuous
Meddle Not Its Unison With The Supreme.

Shivam Sahu

I love poetry and i am simple boy

(1)

Rab Kare Zindagi Mein Aisa Mukaam Aaye,
Meri Rooh Aur Jaan Aapke Kaam Aaye,
Har Dua Mein Bas Yehi Maangte Hain Rab Se,
Ki Agle Janam Mein Bhi Aapke Naam Ke Sath Mera Naam
Aaye..

(2)

Agar Thak Jaao Kabhi Toh Humse Kahna
Hum Utha Lenge Tumko Apni Baahon Mein
Aap Ek Baar Pyar Karke Toh Dekho Humse
Hum Khusiyan Bichha Denge Aapki Raahon Mein

(3)

Kuch Ulje Sawalo Se Darta Hai Dil,
Jane Kyun Tanhai Mein Bikharta Hai Dil,
Kisi Ko Panne Ki Ab Koi Chahat Nahi,
Bas Kuch Apno Ko Khone Se Darta Hai Dil....

Kapil Sahare

Kapil Sahare is a Civil Engineer by profession and Writer by passion. He is hailing from Bhopal (MP) and graduated from UIT RGPV Bhopal. He is a humble and generous person who loves to write his own words what he has within. He is also a Poet, a Novelist, a Nature Lover and an enthusiast contributing to Welfare Works. He's certain that he has the power to change lives for the better. It is his own way to keep himself sane, happy and in love with life. He himself is a practitioner of Vipassana meditation, which constantly inspires him to learn something new, strive for learning and personal development. Insta id : kapilsahare01

अपनों के सपने

"आप कई दिनों से ठीक से सो क्यों नहीं रहे हैं ?" पूनम ने, विशाल से पूछा, जो हर घडी करवटे बदल रहा था, फिर कुछ देर यूँ ही पड़े रहने के बाद वो पलंग पर ही उठकर बैठ गया । थोड़ी देर बाद जब पूनम को उसके बैठे रहने का आभास हुआ, तो वो भी झट से उठकर बैठ गई और विशाल के माथे को छूकर पूछा, "आपकी तबियत तो ठीक हैं न ?"

"हाँ, मैं तो ठीक ही हूँ ।" विशाल बोला, तो पूनम उससे सटकर बैठते हुए बोली, "बताइए न, क्या हुआ ?"

"आपका सपना मुझे सोने नहीं देता ।" उसने बताया, तो पूनम ने माथे पर हाथ लगाते हुए कहा, "छोडिए न उसे, वो तो मैंने ऐसे ही कह दिया था । आप भी न, चलिए सो जाइए जल्दी, कल ऑफिस भी तो जाना हैं न ।"

"नहीं पूनम, अब आपका वो सपना मेरा सपना बन गया हैं, जिसे मैं हर हाल में पूरा करने का प्रयत्न करूँगा ।" विशाल गंभीर होकर अपनी आँखे बंद करते हुए बोला ।

"पापा..." मृणाली ने कमरे में दाखिल होते हुए कहा, तो विशाल आँखे खोलते हुए बोला, "हम्म..?"

"मैंने सुना, आप मम्मा से बात कर रहे थे न ?" मृणाली, विशाल के सीने से चिपककर उसके पास बैठते हुए बोली, तो विशाल की आँखों से आंसू छलक पड़े, फिर उसने प्यार से मृणाली के सिर पर हाथ फेरते हुए बताया, "आपकी मम्मा, हमेशा एक सपना देखा करती थी, मौत को चकमा देकर वापिस जिन्दा होकर अपने पास आने का सपना और मैं उसका सपना पूरा करना चाहता हूँ ।"

"But how can it be possible papa ?..." मृणाली ने उठते हुए कहा, "...आप मम्मा के सपने को इतना Seriously कैसे ले सकते हैं ?"

विशाल कुछ न बोला और चलते सीलिंग फेन की ओर एकटक देखता रहा । मृणाली अपने कमरे में जाकर सो गई और बैठे-बैठे विशाल को भी कब नींद लग गई, पता ही नहीं चला । सुबह होते ही मृणाली ने गरमा-गरम चाय-

नाश्ता तैयार कर डाइनिंग टेबल पर बैठते हुए आवाज़ लगाई, "पापा, नाश्ता करने आ जाइये ।"

मृणाली प्लेट में नाश्ता डालकर कप में चाय भर ही रही थी कि अचानक कमरे से विशाल और पूनम को एकसाथ आता देख भौचक्की सी उन्हें देखती रह गई । उसकी ख़ुशी का कोई ठिकाना नहीं रहा और वो जोर से चीखती हुई उन दोनों की और दौड़ पड़ी । फिर मृणाली जैसे ही उनके गले लगने को हुई, वैसे ही उनकी आत्मा के आर-पार निकल गई और पलंग पर विशाल की मृत देह को देखकर हैरान रह गई । वो अपनी आँखों से आंसुओ की मोटी-मोटी बुँदे गिराती हुई कभी विशाल और पूनम की आत्मा को देखती जा रही थी, तो कभी विशाल की मृत देह को देखकर । भावना में बहकर वो जोर से चीख पड़ी, "पापा..."

जोर की भयानक चीख सुनकर विशाल भागता हुआ मृणाली के कमरे में जा घुसा, जिसे जिन्दा देखकर मृणाली रोते-बिलखते हुए उसके गले लग पड़ी और रोते-रोते ही बोलने लगी, "पा..पापा.. सपना.. सपने में.. सपने में आप दोनों.. आप दोनों.."

Surender Saini

वैसे तो ज़िन्दगी से गिला भी क्या है "उड़ता"
गौर से देखूं तो हुनर से ज़्यादा मिला भी क्या है
सुरेंद्र सैनी बवानीवाल, झज्जर (हरियाणा)के रहने वाले हैं.इनकी शिक्षा b.sc,
B.a, Mba(Hr&marketing), Ll.b honors, Pgdjmc है इनकी लेखनी मुक्त
विचारों पर आधारित है.ये 09 वर्ष की आयु से लिखने का शौक रखते हैं.
इन्होंने अभी तक कविताएं, कहानी, वृतांत, निबंध, तिक्का, स्क्रिप्ट, नाटक
आदि लिखा है

शहर की ऊँची मीनारें...

खा गयी हिस्से की धूप शहर की ऊँची मीनारें
खा गयी मासूम - रूप शहर की ऊँची मीनारें
आजकल सूरज मुझसे कुछ देर से मिलता है
करती रिहायश कुरूप शहर की ऊँची मीनारें
कितनी आवाज़ें दबी,सुनायी नहीं देती हमको
क्यों हमें कर रही चुप शहर की ऊँची मीनारें
यहाँ रहना तो जैसे अपनी मज़बूरी हो गयी है
ज़मीनों को बनाती कूप शहर की ऊँची मीनारें
घर से चले तो अपना एक रुतबा था "उड़ता"
हुए भिखारी यहाँ भूप' शहर की ऊँची मीनारें
(राजा)

ख़्वाब से बढ़कर क्या है

ये जीने का मकसद देता है ख़्वाब से बढ़कर क्या है
दायरों से आगे मंजिल है दोआब से बढ़कर क्या है
देखी जो खूबसूरती उनकी हिज़ाब से बढ़कर क्या है
कायनात में छिपा राज़ कि शबाब से बढ़कर क्या है
कभी उसके हसीन चेहरे पर इताब से बढ़कर क्या है
जब भी तन्हाई में याद आए शराब से बढ़कर क्या है
मज़बूरीयों में भी झुकें क्यों रुआब से बढ़कर क्या है
उसका सवाल कुछ पेचीदा जवाब से बढ़कर क्या है
"उड़ता"अल्फाज़ ये अपने हैं झाब' से बढ़कर क्या है
(टोकरी)

बस तू नहीं है...

सभीकुछ तो है बस तू नहीं है
फल हैं तरु पर रस तू नहीं है
कोई गंध फैली है मेरे कमरे में
हर चीज़ बरबस खुश्बू नहीं है
अहसास तो है भीतरी हवा में
तेरे जिस्म का रक्स-बू नहीं है
मेरा रोम - रोम अकड़ गया है
चाहत का रस जुस्तजू नहीं है
हर तरफ ऊष्मा भरा ताप है
गर्मी बहुत है बेबस लू नहीं है
ख़्वाहिश करें किस चीज़ की
ज़हन फटता पस रफू नहीं है
ख़ामोशी की चादर फैली है
ना कोई रूह - जस सू नहीं है
"उड़ता"खानाबदोश ज़िन्दगी
चलता सा मंजस तम्बू नहीं है

Harkirat Singh

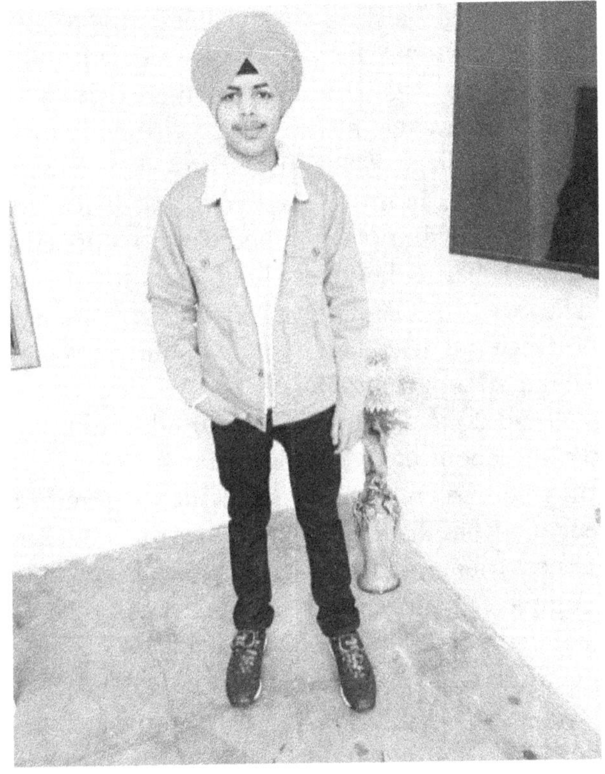

Harkirat Singh, 16 years old, lives in punjab.
He is a passionate writer. He pen down what he feels. He wants to live his life on his own terms and conditions. And he wants to explore his life by improvising his thoughts and words. He has written a book which will publish soon.

Why I Write ?

From the beginning, I always wrote something on my diary... And I have my personal diary where I wrote all my feelings and desire... There was a time when there was nobody to whom I can share my feelings so started writing in my diary... I started writing diary when I was only ten. When I was fourteen a girl came in my life & that girl actually taught me the real meaning of life... When she came I stopped writing diary & started sharing her everything about my life and day-by-day she was influencing me with her thoughts and positivity. Once I realised that living without her is hard when she hurted me by sudden ignorance... It was hard but there was nothing I could do and then again I started writing diary.... I started writing about her... I was broken & confused...... But the person who hurts me so much tells me to write something what i feel and from that day I started to write a book on her... She is my best friend.. I take a year to wrote a book on her and when I completed that book, I send that book to my closest friends and everyone said that book is very awesome... I was in shock and i realized that i can also write... For me writing is not only to write about a topic, for me writing is a feeling which i always felt... Sometimes, I am not comfortable to tell my feelings to someone and that time I used to write.. I write when I saw something wrong, I write when I want to change something, I write when my heart feels something... For me writing is my best friend which I never want to loose.. For me writing is a voice which can change the world...

Dr. Manjusha Hari

A poet and teacher. Doctorate in Malayalam. Residing in Kerala. She published 2 solo poetry collections and 3 anthologies. Writing is her life and passion. Writing to exist and existing to write!

I Was Here

The bubbles of self,
just scattering
over my disappointed desire,
like a prism..
You, the reflection
spreading here,
over my secret sin!
You were here
always..
We, separated
with a river of ego.
A rainbow of revenge,
waiting to be a circle
of fulfillness..
the debt of births flowing,
over my asceticism,
sedately...
a tepid dream emanating
in my hibernation..!

Me?

I am a whirlwind,
among these words,
I am the Enlightenment
of rare wisdom,
I am the pith of papyrus.
I am
the ancient smell
of your caves,
the corpse of your
ancestors,
and the silence reigns
before you !
I am the nip of headiness,
I am the furious battle,
I am the Oracular yammer,
I am the heady land
of life..
and I am the Book of dead,
I am the oblation of self
And I am the lost script !

Flairs and Glairs, a platform by a student for the students. We are esteemed youth struggling to carve out our path for our future and we follow a basic mindset Since everyone is not born with all-round skills. Joining hands with people who are born to execute it with perfection is the best way to evolve. Self-Evolution is the need of the hour but, evolving as a community is what we strive for. The initiative as kickstarted by, Founder- Mr. Shubham Shah with the motive to utilize the skillset and talent of writing has now a team of 10+ people who are actively participating into newer forms of learning and discovering talents among youngsters. We Provide platform and services like Publishing opportunities, Open mics, Workshops, Hands-on training. Operating with Brand Name of Flairs and Glairs (Publication House), we offer the chance of elevating a passionate writer to an esteemed author With Brand name Teekhe Zasbaaat. We bring to you an opportunity to get accustomed with the Public Speaking and Presenting of Thoughts along with regular challenges to brush up your inking spirit. The newest initiative to extend our services we introduced in a new writing Platform- The Glittering Fables and Ink Over Tears.

We Choose to Fly Like A Falcon than to be

a Leg Pulling Crab.

To Know More: Infoline – 7781900870
Mail Us At-
flairsandglairs@gmail.com / info@flairsandglairs.in
Or Visit is at
www.flairsandglairs.com / www.flairsandglairs.in
Social Handles- @flairsandglairs @teekhezasbaaat